Releasing

The Drums

of War

UNDERSTANDING SPIRITUAL
WEAPONS AND WARFARE

LIONEL J. TRAYLOR

ISBN: 9781672019439

DEDICATION

This book is dedicated to My Intercessors and My Spiritual Family. We war and wrestle on each other's behalf.

But VICTORY belongs to JESUS!

ACKNOWLEDGMENTS

First, thanks be unto God from whom all blessings flow. I am grateful to Jesus for giving me life more abundantly and a purpose to live.

Secondly, to my wife and kids, for always supporting me.

To my church family, my family, for all your love and support.

Special thanks are due to my team on this project, the ministers Casandra Ware and Felix Anderson. Thank you both!

Finally, thank you, Bishop RC Blakes, for doing the foreword and for your continued support and friendship. May God continue to bless you, sir.

FOREWORD

Bishop Traylor has done it again. In this latest work, Releasing the Drums of War, he brings us into spiritual dimensions that the church has forfeited. Religions and traditions of men have robbed the Body of Christ of true power.

He reintroduces us to the fact that this is a warfare we're in. Triumphant warfare always begins and ends with a sound. A silent church is a clueless and powerless entity.

The author points out the power we possess in our mouths as believers. Prayer, praise prophecy, and proclamation are weapons that are most effective in releasing glory and dismantling the agenda of darkness.

This is truly a book that brings timeless spiritual disciplines to a fresh generation. It's a generation looking for things divine and spiritually pure. Bishop Traylor is graced to write in a fashion that opens the understanding to deep spiritual truth. Enjoy this journey into the deeper realms. Things will never sound the same.

Bishop R.C. Blakes, Jr.
New Home Family Worship Center

CONTENTS

INTRODUCTION

"There is never a time during warfare, both naturally and spiritually, that you have the luxury of being ignorant. The more informed you are... The more empowered you are."
~Lionel J. Traylor~

Pastor William Murphy III is quoted as saying, "There's always a kingdom sound that proceeds a move of God. Wherever you find a move of God, it is always associated with a sound." This is of a truth even concerning *warfare*. Drums or percussion have great significance in warfare. Historically, they aided in synchronizing the movement of the troops. Due to the loudness of most war zones, certain drum rolls were even used to communicate warnings of attack or the necessity to retreat. *Releasing the Drums of War* highlights the drum's function to dictate the cadence, the rhythm, and the atmosphere during spiritual warfare.

Like it or not, spiritual warfare is a reality in the life of every Christian. It's unavoidable. At some point on your journey, you will be engaged by direct and sometimes not so direct demonic opposition. When that time comes, you need to be prepared. *Releasing the Drums of War* perfectly breaks down the intricate factors of spiritual weaponry and how the believer can effectively utilize them against the enemy. It makes clear the necessity to be sensitive to what we see, hear and speak. We know that we have the victory in Christ Jesus. Yet, we also have a very diligent adversary that is committed to ripping that victory away from us by any means possible. He is relentless. He is determined. He is strongly motivated by his hatred for Christ. Make no mistake, he hates you as well. Therefore, we must be aware not only of his tactics, but what is the totality of our defense; and what weapons are in our arsenal against him.

Be sober, be vigilant; because your adversary the devil, as a roaring lion, walketh about, seeking whom he may devour: 1 Peter 5:8

When we consider war, one must note that there are many sounds heard; sounds of defeat, sounds of death, sounds of life, and sounds of victory. However, there are four sounds heard in spiritual warfare that are crucial for the believer to discern, understand the operation of and properly activate if victory is to be achieved. Those sounds are Praise, Prayer, Prophecy, and Proclamation. Praise is for God, Prayer is for you, Prophecy is for strategy, and Proclamation is for the witnesses.

View *Releasing the Drums of War* as a quick guide, a checklist, if you will, to be used to sharpen your mindset and strengthen your resolve concerning spiritual warfare. The reader should gain greater insight on the primary elements and sounds of warfare, understand when and how our weapons should be released, and receive strategy for how you can be more effective in warfare, coming out successful and victorious every time!

Casandra Ware
Azania Creations LLC
Owner/Operator

DRUM OF PRAISE

"Choose to engage in Warfare strategically.

It's not about giving a RESPONSE

but gaining REWARDS."

~Lionel J. Traylor~

A Noise in The Camp

And Moses turned and went down from the mount, and the two tables of the testimony were in his hand: the tables were written on both their sides; on the one side and on the other were they written. And the tables were the work of God, and the writing was the writing of God, graven upon the tables. And when Joshua heard the noise of the people as they shouted, he said unto Moses, there is *A NOISE OF WAR* in the camp. And he said, It is not the voice of them that shout for mastery, neither is it the voice of them that cry for being overcome: but the noise of them that sing (praise & worship) do I hear. **Exodus 32:15-18**

PRAISE: *Commendation bestowed on a person for his personal virtues or worthy actions, to do honor to; to express gratitude for personal favors.*

U pon evaluation of the text, we can see that this was not a season of bondage for the children of Israel. They had been freed from the slavery of Pharaoh and Egypt. In fact, they were in a season of prophetic promotion. Before you get to see your complete vision manifested, elevation and promotion are a perfect time to praise God for what he has already done on your behalf. God instructs Moses to come up the mountain so he could reveal his glory and give him prophetic instructions. God's glory is not just an abstract thing but is attainable, and once upon us, it leads and directs us into places we have never experienced before. It makes no sense to get revelation and not get instruction. It makes no sense to receive divine prophecy, and it does not point you in the direction you need to go. So, God releases prophecy and promotion and requires but one thing in return, praise.

Consider Harvest Season (Promotion Season) is also our haunting season because it is usually when we are tempted and tested the most. As the children of Israel arrived at the mountain of God to receive divine instructions, when they should have been giving him praise for what he had brought them through, Moses heard a noise coming from the camp. While Moses was getting fresh vision from God on the mountain, the people had moved into witchcraft, rebellion, idolatry, and paganism. Moses heard *praise,* but because it was unto idol gods, Joshua heard warfare!

Praise is not something one would commonly associate with warfare. I'd say that's because most people don't know how powerful their praise is. Praise invokes God's presence. It's like a spiritual honing device bringing him to your location. David said it this way in Psalm 22, "But thou art holy, O thou that inhabitest the praises of Israel." Another translation says that God "dwells" in our praises. That means he lives in our praises. When we praise and worship our God, he shows up! Regardless of how we feel, God is worthy of and deserves our praise. A true relationship with him denotes that we praise God for who he is, not for what he's done.

How then could something so positive be considered a weapon. Easily. Your praise to God is a seething war cry in the ears of the devil! In fact, it's confrontational to him. It confuses the kingdom of darkness (2 Chronicles 20:22). Therefore, it is a very effective weapon in your spiritual arsenal.

Your sincere praise will strangle the necks of your enemies! Your enemies can't breathe in the midst of your praise because Satan cannot inhabit the same atmosphere as God. God steps in, and devils step out. Shout for your victory in advance!

Three Times Praise Is A Weapon Against You

1. **Idolatry-** *praising and worshiping things other than God.*
   - It will cost you the kingdom. Matthew 19:16–30
   - Anything other than the worship of God sounds like war against the kingdom of God. Exodus 20:3-5
   - False worship can only produce wilderness in your life.

2. **Self-Worship-** *allowing adoration of others to exalt you.*
   - Don't allow the praise and worship of people to be exalted above God. John 12:43
   - The praise of man will put you in a bad place with God. The enemy will use the approval of people to get you out of God's will. Luke 6:26
   - The praise and worship of men will drive you to witchcraft. 1 Samuel 28:3-25

- Sounds good to you, but it sounds like warfare to God. Acts 16:16, Acts 12:23, 1 Peter 5:6
- It will disqualify you for your harvest and knocks off your throne! Acts 12:23

3. **Inability to Discern Difference Between Praise and War-***confused about what season you are in.*
   - You need to be able to distinguish the sounds.
   - You can't afford to confuse your seasons of war and peace.
   - You need to be able to properly translate the sound of the trumpets of warning. 1 Corinthians 14:8.

Moses' instructions were to bring God's people out of Egypt so that they could freely praise and worship Him in the wilderness. Unfortunately, the people began to worship  Baal. We can conclude, therefore, that right after

God promotes you, the enemy's design is to pervert you. Satan wants us so lost in fleshy idolic praise and worship that we are too distracted to prepare for warfare, but God is seeking those that will worship and praise him in spirit and truth. That's when you will realize your victory! Release the drums of your highest praise!

FORTIFYING YOUR PRAISE ARSENAL

⊣— Praise is an instrument of war.

⊣— You need to be able to distinguish the sounds of every season. You need to discern the sounds coming from the people in your camp.

⊣— It is possible to have people in your camp releasing praise and worship that is warring against your destiny.

⊣— Your enemy hears your praise and initiates warfare.

➤ Your celebration is an invitation for demonic attention.

➤ When you're praising, you are glorifying God and simultaneously evicting demonic presence!

➤ Your enemy's goal is to confuse you in order to get you to forfeit what you're supposed to be producing. He intends to get you off focus.

➤ You need to know what season you're in and properly discern what's going on in the spirit realm.

➤ The sounds of the enemy are contradictory to what God is saying over your life. It is a noise to distract destiny. His goal is to disrupt your atmosphere. Guard your ears!

➤ It's the enemy's design that right after God promotes you, Satan tries to pervert. He waits at the foot of your mountain.

➤ Your praise is a sacrificial offering. We don't praise because we feel like it. We praise because God is worthy, and it provides a wall of defense.

✦ Praise positions you for God's glory.
✦ The enemy uses perverted praise and worship to distract your atmosphere so he can keep you from receiving your vision.

TAKEAWAYS

1. How is my praise a weapon against the enemy?
2. What if you don't feel like praising? **(Hebrews 13:15)**
3. When is praise a weapon against me?
4. How important is it to discern the sounds of each season?

WAR KEY

Know your enemies!! Don't just write them off! Especially if they have declared you as an enemy. Know why they are your enemy, so you can understand the area of their warfare and weapons they will use."

LET'S PRAY

Father, it is a privilege and an honor to praise you. It's my desire to worship you. You alone are worthy. You sit high, and you look low. I give you glory that you are the great I am. You are the all-powerful, all-knowing, all-seeing, everlasting God. You are mighty to save! Who can make war with my God? You are the Lord God strong, great, and mighty in battle! Your name is high and lifted up. Arise, oh Lord, and let your enemies be scattered! In you, I find strength. In you, I find joy. In you, I have victory!

I need your presence, Lord. I need your spirit. I need your glory to fill my atmosphere. I cannot and will not move without you, father. You are El Shaddai, Elohim, a strong tower, and the lifter of my hands! You are a fire by night, cloud by day, leading, guiding, and protecting me from hurt and harm! I stand in awe of your faithfulness. Your grace and mercies leave me speechless! Stand up for me, my God. Lift up a standard against those that oppose and conspire against me. Let not my enemies rejoice one minute in my misfortune. Move by your spirit now on behalf of your servant like only you can. And I will give you all the glory, all the honor, and all the praise! For you are worthy!

In Jesus' name, AMEN!

PRAISE AS A WEAPON IN SCRIPTURE

JOSHUA 6:15-21: *And it came to pass on the seventh day, that they rose early about the dawning of the day and compassed the city after the same manner seven times: only on that day they compassed the city seven times. 16 And it came to pass at the seventh time when the priests blew with the trumpets, Joshua said unto the people, Shout; for the Lord hath given you the city.17 And the city shall be accursed, even it, and all that are therein, to the Lord: only Rahab the harlot shall live, she and all that are with her in the house, because she hid the messengers that we sent.18 And ye, in any wise keep yourselves from the accursed thing, lest ye make yourselves accursed, when ye take of the accursed thing, and make the camp of Israel a curse, and trouble it.19 But all the silver, and gold, and vessels of brass and iron, are consecrated unto the Lord: they shall come into the treasury of the Lord.20 So the people shouted when the priests blew with the trumpets: and it came to pass, when the people heard the sound of the trumpet, and the people shouted with a great shout, that the wall fell down flat, so that the people went up into the city, every man straight before him, and they took the city. 21*

And they utterly destroyed all that was in the city, both man and woman, young and old, and ox, and sheep, and ass, with the edge of the sword.

2 CHRONICLES 20:20-24: *And they rose early in the morning and went forth into the wilderness of Tekoa: and as they went forth, Jehoshaphat stood and said, Hear me, O Judah, and ye inhabitants of Jerusalem; Believe in the Lord your God, so shall ye be established; believe his prophets, so shall ye prosper. 21 And when he had consulted with the people, he APPOINTED SINGERS unto the Lord, and that should praise the beauty of holiness, as they went out before the army, and to say, Praise the Lord; for his mercy endureth forever. 22 And WHEN THEY BEGAN TO SING AND TO PRAISE, the Lord set ambushments against the children of Ammon, Moab, and mount Seir, which were come against Judah; and they were smitten. 23 For the children of Ammon and Moab stood up against the inhabitants of mount Seir, utterly to slay and destroy them: and when they had made an end of the inhabitants of Seir, everyone helped to destroy another. 24 And when Judah came toward the watch tower in the wilderness, they looked unto the multitude, and, behold, they were dead bodies fallen to the earth, and none escaped.*

Further Study: 2 Kings 3:12-18, 1 Samuel 16:15-23

DRUM OF PRAYER

"You can never conquer or change what you ignorantly or willfully refuse to acknowledge."

~Lionel J. Traylor~

A Noise from The Wall

So, *BUILT WE THE WALL*; and all the wall was joined together unto the half thereof: for the people had a mind to work. But it came to pass, that when Sanballat, and Tobiah, and the Arabians, and the Ammonites, and the Ashdodites, heard that the walls of *Jerusalem* were made up, and that the breaches began to be stopped, then they were very wroth, And *CONSPIRED ALL OF THEM TOGETHER* to come and to fight against Jerusalem, and to hinder it. *NEVERTHELESS, WE MADE OUR PRAYER* unto our God, and *SET A WATCH* against them *DAY AND NIGHT*, because of them. **Nehemiah 4:6-10**

PRAYER: *A sincere request for help or expression of thanks communicated with God.*

Watch and Pray: Spiritual Warfare Prayers

The church was birthed in prayer. The most important ministry in the church after Proclamation is Intercession. Intercessors repair the breach. They stop up all the holes in the wall. In fact, if you want to have a strong church, you need intercessors! If you don't have any walls, you don't have any defense. Without walls, anything can come in. It doesn't matter how strong you are internally, if you don't have external protection. It'll only be a matter of time before the enemy comes in and causes damage. You need *gates* and *walls;* you need *protection.*

Nehemiah and the people were rebuilding the city's wall peacefully until their enemies *heard* about it. When their enemies heard that they were attempting to strengthen themselves, have peace, prosper, and rebuild the walls, they were grieved. If you are ever going to prosper in your life, you are going to need a wall. Your enemy does not mind you having peace as long as your "peace" is under the hand of bondage.

Likewise, your enemy does not mind your religious repetitive (ineffective) prayers. He's concerned with your fervent, faith-filled prayers that move you into a position for war

Our fervent prayers provoke God to move on our behalf!

against him. Your bold warfare prayers of faith have a different sound in the ears of enemies than timid religious begging.

If you are in a place in your walk where you are trying to rebuild your walls, be mindful that ALL of your enemies are on alert. Anytime your prayers start to provoke prosperity and peace in your life, they also are invoking warfare from your enemies! Consider all of your prayers are not warfare prayers. Some prayers can build you up but leave you vulnerable. Those are prayers that are internal and will never affect anything externally in your life. This is considered ineffective prayer. What are you saying in your prayers? In the natural, everyone that goes into a gym does not properly know how to exercise for optimum results. It is the same in prayer. Your prayers must be discerned. All prayers must have a purpose. All prayers must have a target.

When the enemy hears that you are attempting to rebuild your life, he's not just going to sit quietly. Never forget, he comes to kill, steal, and *destroy*! His assignment is to finish what he started, and that is to drag you back into the bondage you came out of. Your enemy's strategy is to fight you up close and from afar. He wants to make you feel surrounded and overwhelmed, so you stop building your wall. But don't get distracted. Focus on your task (Nehemiah 4:9)!

To truly be effective in warfare prayer, you need to identify your prayer watch (Habakkuk 2:1). A prayer watch is a particular time of day or night when your prayers are most effective. There are different prayers for every watch. There are eight prayer watches in three-hour increments, starting at six o'clock in the evening. Do you know your prayer watch? If you plan to be effective in warfare prayer, you need to know your watch, and your prayer language needs to come up to the level where heaven moves on your behalf. Can your prayers shift atmospheres?

Jesus gave us a good point of reference in Matthew 6:9-13. Most people simply repeat this prayer verbatim. That was not the intended use.

He began with, "Our father which art in heaven.", meaning you can not get a prayer through without beginning with praise. Jesus was showing us how to gain access to answered prayers. Praise provokes God's presence. And one should not go into the presence of God and not know who he is nor believes that he answers the prayers of his children. Your prayer life is a weapon. Do you know how to pray and get an answer?

Do you understand the operation of your prayer weapons? Your fervent prayers are fiery darts against the enemy. They are a part of your armor (Ephesians 6:16-18). Your enemy's tactics include fighting with you in close combat, which gives you an opportunity to use your sword (the Word of God), but he also attacks from a distance. What do I do about attacks from afar? I pull out my arrows! Your warfare prayers are fiery arrows against the enemy. From the tower, a place of elevation, you can take proper aim to inflict devastating blows. Are you ready? Properly dressed and armed for war, you can then declare: *"Don't make yourself my enemy unless you want to fight with my God!"*

Three Places Warfare Prayers are Effective

1. **The Wall**: Position of strength and elevation (Faith & Righteousness). Psalm 64:1, Joel 3:10

2. **The Watch**: Knowing what time and place where you are the most effective in warfare prayer.

3. **The Word**: If you don't know how to use the word of God in prayer, you will be ineffective on the wall and on your watch. Your words are weapons. You have to know how to use them.

FORTIFYING YOUR PRAYER ARSENAL

➤ Your prayers protect you from your enemies.

➤ When you build the walls, you get peace. Jerusalem means extended peace.

➤ Your enemy will fight close up and from a distance. His goal is to stop you from building your wall.

➤ Your enemy wants to take your peace and give you problems until you get so tired you just walk away and quit. Daniel 7:25

> *You will never be effective against an enemy you don't know! Know thy ENEMY!*

➤ The enemy hears when you're trying to build yourself up. How do I build myself up? Jude 20 (KJV) But ye, beloved, ***building up*** yourselves on your most holy faith, ***praying*** in the Holy Ghost,

➵ It's not a prayer if you can't open your mouth and utter it. If it's not spoken, it's not a request. Saying it in your mind is meditation, not supplication or intercession.

➵ If I'm praying *ineffectively*, I can't move any mountains!

➵ Your prayers must be *effective*. Your prayers must be discerned. You can be praying in error and asking God amidst. James 4:2-3.

➵ Your prayers can be hindered by a contaminated atmosphere. Daniel 10:12

➵ If I do not have an effective prayer life, then I do not have an open communication line with God!

➵ It's illegal for me to pray before I praise God.

➵ Your prayers are your arrows, but you have to be on your watch to shoot them

➤ From the wall, the watchman warns the people when the enemies are approaching.

➤ The wall represents a place of elevation. From a place of elevation, I'm able to better aim my prayers.

➤ The enemy doesn't want you to know prayer is part of your armor.

TAKEAWAYS

1. What exactly does *fervent prayer* mean?
2. What part does prayer represent in my spiritual armor?
3. How do I know when I'm most effective in prayer?
4. What kind of prayers invoke fear in the enemy?
5. Why is my position on the watchtower important to my weapon of prayer?
6. Are warfare prayers, petitions, and supplications the same?

WAR KEY

"If we preach biblical obedience without the biblical blessings of obedience, we are teaching the faithful to engage in a warfare that has no benefits or reward."

LET US PRAY

Father, teach my hands how to war. You have not given me a spirit of fear; endow me now to be bold as a lion in this season of my life. In you alone do I place my trust! I put you in remembrance of your word. You said your word would not return unto you void, but it shall accomplish everything you sent it out to do. You said no weapon fashioned or formed against me shall prosper. You said you would make my enemies your enemies. You said with my own eyes, I would see the reward of the wicked. You said your angels wait to perform your word. I now command the angels that you have given charge over my life to war in the natural and war in the spirit victoriously on my behalf. I command every demonic trap, set up, sabotage, every demonic regime, and every demonic allegiance laid up for me and joined together against me to be destroyed in the name of Jesus. May confusion be in their borders. May every demonic spy and information gatherer be deaf and blind to my movements. Let everything hidden in darkness be exposed. Let every curse be uprooted. Let every yoke be destroyed, and every burden be lifted out of my life! It will work out for my good. I will have victory. I will overcome. In Jesus' name, AMEN!

Bible Based Warfare Prayers

Psalm 35: 1-9

Plead my cause, O Lord, with them that strive with me: fight against them that fight against me. 2 Take hold of shield and buckler and stand up for mine help. 3 Draw out also the spear, and stop the way against them that persecute me: say unto my soul, I am thy salvation.4 Let them be confounded and put to shame that seek after my soul: let them be turned back and brought to confusion that devise my hurt.5 Let them be as chaff before the wind: and let the angel of the Lord chase them.6 Let their way be dark and slippery: and let the angel of the Lord persecute them.7 For without cause have they hid for me their net in a pit, which without cause they have digged for my soul. 8 Let destruction come upon him at unawares; and let his net that he hath hid catch himself: into that very destruction let him fall. 9 And my soul shall be joyful in the Lord: it shall rejoice in his salvation.

Psalm 91:1-12

He that dwelleth in the secret place of the most High shall abide under the shadow of the Almighty. 2 I will say of the Lord, He is my refuge and my fortress: my God; in him will I trust. 3

Surely, he shall deliver thee from the snare of the fowler, and from the noisome pestilence. 4 He shall cover thee with his feathers, and under his wings shalt thou trust: his truth shall be thy shield and buckler. 5 Thou shalt not be afraid for the terror by night; nor for the arrow that flieth by day; 6 Nor for the pestilence that walketh in darkness; nor for the destruction that wasteth at noonday. 7 A thousand shall fall at thy side, and ten thousand at thy right hand; but it shall not come nigh thee. 8 Only with thine eyes shalt thou behold and see the reward of the wicked. 9 Because thou hast made the Lord, which is my refuge, even the most High, thy habitation; 10 There shall no evil befall thee, neither shall any plague come nigh thy dwelling. 11 For he shall give his angels charge over thee, to keep thee in all thy ways. 12 They shall bear thee up in their hands, lest thou dash thy foot against a stone.

Psalms 64:1 *Hear my voice, O God, in my prayer: preserve my life from fear of the enemy. Hide me from the **secret counsel of the wicked**; from the insurrection of the workers of iniquity: Who whet their tongue like a sword, and bend their bows to shoot their arrows, even bitter words: That they may shoot in secret at the perfect: suddenly do* *they shoot at him, and fear not. They encourage themselves in an evil matter: they commune of laying snares privily; they say,* **Who shall see them***? They search out iniquities; they accomplish a diligent search: both the inward thought of every one of them, and the heart, is deep.* **But God shall shoot at them** *with an* **ARROW;** *suddenly shall they be wounded. So, they shall make their own tongue to fall upon themselves: all that see them shall flee away. And* **all men shall fear and shall declare the work of God; for they shall wisely consider of his doing***. The righteous shall be glad in the Lord and shall trust in him; and all the upright in heart shall glory.*

For Further Study: Psalm 54, 2 Chronicles 20:5-12

DRUM OF PROPHECY

"If you are more confused after the prophecy than before the prophecy... It wasn't God."

~Lionel J. Traylor~

Blow the Trumpet in Zion

Again the word of the Lord came unto me, saying, Son of man, *SPEAK* to the children of thy people, and say unto them, When I bring the sword upon a land, if the people of the land take a man of their coasts, and set him for their *WATCHMAN*: If when he seeth the sword come upon the land, he *BLOWS THE TRUMPET*, and *WARN THE PEOPLE*; Then *WHOSOEVER HEARETH* the sound of the trumpet, and taketh not warning; if the sword comes, and take him away, his blood shall be upon his own head. He heard the sound of the trumpet and took not warning; his blood shall be upon him. But he that taketh warning shall deliver his soul. But if the watchman sees the sword come, and *BLOW NOT THE TRUMPET*, and the people be not warned; if the sword comes, and take any person from among them, he is taken away in his iniquity; but *HIS BLOOD WILL I REQUIRE AT THE WATCHMAN'S HAND*. So, thou, O son of man, I have

SET THEE A WATCHMAN unto the house of Israel; therefore, thou shalt hear the word at my mouth and warn them from me. (**Ezekiel 33:1-7**).

> **PROPHECY**: *An inspired utterance, something that is declared by a prophet, especially a divinely inspired prediction.*

No King Goes to War Without First Consulting the Prophet

It's amazing that the church, which is a spiritual entity, has become so spiritually insensitive. We wrestle not against flesh and blood, yet most of us are so distracted by physical fleshy opposition that we have taken our eyes off our true adversary, Satan. Your true enemy is not the coworker gossiping about you at the water cooler.

Your enemy is tactical. Satan is a strategist. He has a plan of attack customized just for you in the areas where he thinks he can win. He waits to make his move

> *Prophecy is a spiritual weapon lying dormant in the arsenals of many saints!*

against you in seasons of weakness or great trials; then, he attacks you. He waits until your walls are down. He waits until you lose your job.

He waits until you're having issues in your marriage or with your children. He knows when you're not operating with a strategy. That's when he attacks.

This is why prophecy is a necessary weapon in the arsenal of warfare. While prayer is from you to God, prophecy is from God to you. Prophecy reveals. Prophecy gives revelation.

The sword of the spirit, which is the word of God, is your weapon for combat. Anytime you say what God says, you are *prophesying*. The sword (the word of God) is ineffective unless it is released from your mouth.

> *But what saith it? The word is nigh thee, even in thy mouth, and in thy heart: that is, the word of faith, which we preach; word is nigh thee.* **Romans 10:8-10 KJV**

You do warfare with your mouth! BUT... you can't say what you want to say. You must say what God says to be truly effective in battle. Therefore, I must *know* what he said. If I'm simply repeating religious jargon that has no root in God's word, then I'm basically carrying around a dull sword. For this cause, many saints are living defeated. The word of God (Sword) in your mouth is the spirit of prophecy. Paul suggested not to despise prophesying (1 Thessalonians 5:20-21) because he understood prophecy is a weapon against our enemies. If God said it, then it so! There is no success in spiritual warfare without the shekinah glory of God or the prophetic.

Prophet Ezekiel The Watchman
Four Important Things to Understand

Ezekiel, a major prophet whose name means "God will strengthen", ever had his ear to the mouth of God. A prophet, unlike the priest, prepares you to engage in warfare.

1. God Tells Ezekiel To SPEAK (Ezekiel 33:2): Prophecy is giving warning. This prophetic voice is preparing them for a battle to come. Your enemy doesn't give you a warning; your watchman (prophet) does. A prophetic word gives you the when, the where, the who, and the why of your situation. You need instructions during warfare.

2. He is a WATCHMAN (Ezekiel 33:7): There must be a watchman. The watch is a place of prayer, but also a place of prophecy. After I pray, I must wait and listen for God to respond, which is the spirit of prophecy. Whenever God speaks a divine utterance, it is the spirit of prophecy. It is therefore not prophesying until you say what he said. Permission to release is for the office of a prophet or to have prophetic moments to operate in the spirit of prophecy. For example,

Saul was not a prophet, but he prophesied while in the atmosphere of prophets (1 Samuel 10:6,1 Samuel 19:21-24). He never prophesied when he was not with the prophets. That would be out of order, as he was not a prophet. This helped Saul be victorious in battle. Warfare became easy for Saul as long as he could hear from God and had a prophetic voice. Warfare was only hard for Saul when he had no prophetic voice. Understand that at that point, God had commanded his prophets not to speak to Saul. Like Saul, many Christians are losing battles because pride has come into their hearts, and they refuse to follow prophetic instructions.

In warfare, you definitely need a watchman. The watchman holds value because they see and know what you cannot. He is positioned high and is a *seer*. He sees danger first, from afar (foreknowledge), so he can warn and instruct. Every nation needs a watchman. Every state needs a watchman. Every city needs a watchman. Every family needs a watchman.

Consequently, because the watchman sees danger first, they are also the first to be targeted. So, a watchman must be strong, disciplined, and set apart so that he or she may be effective in their position.

3. **He must sound the TRUMPET (Ezekiel 33:3)**: The trumpet is not only used for warning. There is a Sound of Worship, War, and Victory.

4. **His WORDS (Ezekiel 33:5-6)**: Words of warning flow from the mouth of the prophet. His words must come from the mouth of God to his ear and then from his mouth to the ears of the people and is then released by the listeners.

There are four categories for the words released by the watchman.

1.   Words of Warning
2.   Words of Instructions
3.   Words of Inspiration
4.   Words of Strategy

The weapon of prophecy stops the weapon of self-destruction! The bible says a man's way is right in his own eyes (Proverbs 21:2-4); therefore, I cannot watch for myself. I need someone else who does not have the bias I have about *myself* (self-righteousness) to watch for me.

Crucial Functions of Prophecy in Warfare

1. Prophecy lets you know what your enemy is planning against you! (Luke 14:31)
2. Prophecy lets you know what weapons are effective against your enemies. (2 Corinthians 10:4, 2 Corinthians 2:11)

3. Prophecy lets you know who is for you and who is against you. It will reveal who your enemy is even in your camp. (Jeremiah 33:3, Jeremiah 11:18)

4. Prophecy gives you strategy (Proverbs 24:6)

The Significance of The Tower

The tower functions as protection and a place to house the goods. It represents vital communication. Before the enemy attacks anything else, he targets communication. Satan wants to confuse the communication between the tower and the people. He desires to distort the sound. If there's no communication between you and heaven, you will get discouraged because you can't see what's coming and can't get instructions from a confused, distorted source.

In warfare, you need prophetic communication that warns you but also inspires you to keep fighting and not give up. You also need a sensitive discerning ear and an obedient spirit to properly assimilate what's being released. The weapon of prophecy ensures your victory. To ignore or miss it is a costly mistake.

FORTIFYING YOUR PROPHETIC ARSENAL

⟶ Prophecy is a necessary weapon in the arsenal of man because often, we don't hear that an attack is coming.

⟶ It's possible to be very religious yet be very ineffective. You cannot go to warfare ignorant. Your enemy is a strategist. (1 Peter 5:8)

⟶ It makes no sense to get prophecy and not receive principles!

⊷ When God releases prophecy, he doesn't just point; he provides. He doesn't just give glory he guides.

⊷ The enemy wants to break communication between you and heaven. He aims to destroy the tower.

⊷ The enemy is constantly strategizing against you. He's taking account of your strengths and your weakness. The enemy knows your weaknesses better than you know your own strength!

⊷ The enemy wants to ensure that your seeds are uprooted, your faith is discouraged, and your mentality is despondent.

⊷ The watchman stands on the wall, positioned in the tower. The tower is a position of strength and defense. Proverbs 18:10

⊷ You need a watchman who's not too familiar with you and who will speak and reveal the truth.

TAKEAWAYS

1. What role does prophecy play in warfare?
2. What is the primary function of the watchman?
3. Who is the watchman for your house?
4. What qualifies the watchman?
5. What happens when the watchman fails to do their assignment?
6. What does the tower represent? What is its function?

WAR KEY

"The Mind is the battleground for most spiritual warfare. Demonic Suggestions and Spiritual Oppression are seeds sown and rooted into the mind by the enemy. If you lose your mind, you have lost the battle. Manipulation and Deception are the number one tools of the enemies. Though I still yet contend... The WORST kind of DECEPTION is SELF-DECEPTION."

LET US PRAY

Powerful God, Holy God, Righteous God, once again, we come boldly to ask that you release divine insight and divine instructions to your people concerning your heart in this season. Be Father, great light in the darkness! We wish not to operate in error but with sincere desire hope to partake in your next great move! Reveal yourself, oh God. Pour out fresh oil. Pour out fresh revelation. Pour our pure vision, that we may understand the breadth, the height, and the width of your love and purpose in your plan.

Give us ears to hear, eyes to see, a heart to receive, and a spirit to obey what you are saying in the spirit in this season. Let sensitivity and maturity be our portion. Cut off all hindrances, all blockage, and every distraction that would cause us to be confused about your will. Break off rebellious and stiff-necked attitudes. Break off chains of confusion and complaining. Transform mindsets. Let your divine will be done in this hour. Strive with those who strive against us. Per your word, may there be no peace for the wicked. Let an all-consuming fire fall on those that oppose you and accost your children. May turnaround be made manifest right now in the mighty name of Jesus, AMEN!

PROPHECY IN WARFARE

2 Kings 3:10-18: *And the king of Israel said, Alas! That the L*ORD *hath called these three kings together, to deliver them into the hand of Moab! But Jehoshaphat said, Is there not here a prophet of the L*ORD*, that we may enquire of the L*ORD *by him? And one of the kings of Israel's servants answered and said, Here is Elisha the son of Shaphat, which poured water on the hands of Elijah. And Jehoshaphat said, The word of the L*ORD *is with him. So, the king of Israel and Jehoshaphat and the king of Edom went down to him· And Elisha said unto the king of Israel, What have I to do with thee? Get thee to the prophets of thy father and to the prophets of thy mother. And the king of Israel said unto him, Nay: for the L*ORD *hath called these three kings together, to deliver them into the hand of Moab. And Elisha said, As the L*ORD *of hosts liveth, before whom I stand, surely, were it not that I regard the presence of Jehoshaphat the king of Judah, I would not look toward thee, nor see thee. But now bring me a minstrel. And it came to pass, when the minstrel played, that the hand of the L*ORD *came upon him. And he said, Thus saith the L*ORD*, Make this valley full of ditches. For thus saith the L*ORD*, Ye shall not see wind, neither shall ye see rain; yet* *that valley shall be filled with water, that ye may drink, both ye, and your cattle, and your beasts. And this is but a light thing in the sight of the LORD: he will deliver the Moabites also into your hand.*

1 Kings 17:1 *And Elijah the Tishbite, who was of the inhabitants of Gilead, said unto Ahab, As the Lord God of Israel liveth, before whom I stand, there shall not be dew nor rain these years, but according to my word.*

FURTHER STUDY: Deuteronomy 28, Exodus 8

DRUM OF PROCLAMATION

"There will be Glory AFTER THIS!

Your BEST DAYS are still ahead of YOU!

Decree it and Declare it!

Believe it and Receive it!"

~Lionel J. Traylor~

A Declaration of Victory

When thou goest out to battle against thine enemies, and seest horses, and chariots, and a people more than thou, *BE NOT AFRAID OF THEM*: for the *LORD, THY GOD IS WITH THEE*, which brought thee up out of the land of Egypt. And it shall be when ye are come nigh unto the battle, that the priest shall approach and *SPEAK UNTO THE PEOPLE*, And shall say unto them, Hear, O Israel, ye approach this day unto battle against your enemies: let not your hearts faint, fear not, and do not tremble, neither be ye terrified because of them; For the Lord, your God is he that goeth with you, to *FIGHT FOR YOU* against your enemies, *TO SAVE YOU*. **Deuteronomy 20:1-4**

PROCLAMATION: *A public or official announcement, especially one dealing with a matter of great importance.*

No blood-washed believer enters into warfare without a real expectation for a victorious outcome. Your victory, however, is contingent not only on what you believe or what you do before, during, and after the battle, but it is greatly dependent on what you *say*. Proclamation, declaration, and decrees are critical in warfare, and they must be released by someone who has been authorized by God. There are many people speaking things without authority from a God they don't know (Jeremiah 14:14-16)

To declare is to proclaim, and neither can be done quietly. They must be released openly and publicly. A decree is an official statement that something *must* happen. An individual making such a bold statement is indicative that they have been authorized by someone of great power and position, a king, for example. When you make a decree, the enemy sees you as an official representation of the king. The higher you rank in the spirit, that's the level of attack you attract.

Consider that if you are releasing a decree of victory, the enemy automatically hears it as warfare. This is why the enemy wants to shut our mouths. He wants to stop our praise, silence our prayers, confuse our prophecy, and destroy the drum of proclamation. Your voice is sending out a distinct sound to everyone in your camp listening. It is critical in times of warfare that you not only watch what you say but that when you speak, you decree (Job 22:28) the prophecy, precepts, and promises of God.

The sound of victory is trumpeted twice in warfare. Right before the battle, we must proclaim victory within the camp and before our enemy. You can't go into battle quietly. "What needs to be proclaimed as we go into battle?", you may ask. Here's a suggestion. Stand firm and boldly proclaim in the proximity of your enemy, "I'M COMING FOR YOUR HEAD!" That's a good place to start. Don't be surprised or deterred if your enemy begins to release counter proclamations in an effort to distract and frighten you. Consider here the story of David and Goliath (1 Samuel 17). If you really want to make sure God gets into your battle, proclaim it (1 Samuel 17:45-46). The second time the trumpet is blown is after the battle in testimony that God has indeed given you the victory just as he said.

When God gives you a victory, it is so important that you give him the glory (Psalm 106:7). He wants it to be known publicly that he is mighty in battle! Every believer should happily proclaim God's goodness, especially in warfare. We should be swift to proclaim that he is a deliverer! We should be swift to proclaim that he is a provider! We should be swift to proclaim that he is mighty to save! It is an insult to God to come out of an intense spiritual war victoriously and not give him glory. It's spiritually illegal for God to give you victory after victory, and you refuse to blow your trumpet! This is significant for two reasons. First, it reminds Satan that he is defeated while reminding us (believers) that we have victory in Christ. Secondly, your triumphant victory serves as a magnet for non-believers. When you proclaim of God's goodness in warfare, to a non-believer, you are saying come taste and see that my God is good! This validates the importance of proclamation as a weapon.

Drums and Trumpets

You cannot go to war without trumpets and drums. Trumpets are voices. Drums (belly) are the spirit. Therefore, if my voice is the trumpet and my belly is the drum, they both carry the

*Cry aloud,
spare not, lift
up thy voice
like a trumpet*

Isaiah 58:1

sounds of war. So, whatever the drum does, the trumpet must follow. They are on one accord, and they operate in harmony. Their unified *sound* signals different alerts in warfare. Without sounding the trumpet and beating the drum, the people in your camp will be aimless and won't know what to do. More importantly, the enemy, without the sound, is not frightened by your coming.

PROCLAMATION: I proclaim my victory! I will not lose another battle. God is with me! He fights for me! AMEN!

FORTIFYING YOUR PROCLAMATION & DECLARATION ARSENAL

➤ A proclamation is spoken before the battle, and the word of the Lord should be proclaimed publicly and carried by someone with authority, an official.

➤ People are decreeing, declaring, and proclaiming but have no authority. You must be authorized to make a proclamation! Jeremiah 23:21-40

➤ Once you've received your prophecy, then you can proclaim what you heard.

➤ It must be done openly. Many proclaim or decree it privately because they're not sure God said it.

➤ When you make a decree, your enemy hears it as a declaration of war.

━ Know Thy Enemy and His Tactics

- Ambushments (traps and set up)
- Deception (lies, untruths, falsehood, counterfeiting)
- Enticement (Seduction)
- Confusion (Disorder, Chaos)
- Intimidation (Fear causing you to doubt God and his promises)

━ Your voice is sounding (trumpeting) your warfare. It's establishing your reality. 2 Corinthians 10:5, Proverbs 18:21

━ You can't go into battle quiet.

━ Many people are still in the cycle of warfare because he can't trust you to give God the GLORY!

TAKEAWAYS

1. Who has the authority to make a proclamation on behalf of God?
2. Why does a proclamation or decree need to be made publicly?
3. How does it make God feel when we don't testify of his goodness in our victory?

4. What happens if there's no proclamation or declaration made during warfare?

WAR KEY

"Pick Your Battles Wisely. Ask yourself three questions before going to war: 1.) Are the odds in my favor? 2.) What am I willing to sacrifice to engage this enemy? 3.) What will I gain if I am victorious? Or if I lose... what have I lost?"

LET US PRAY

Lord, I give you glory that your word says I can have whatsoever I say and that I can decree a thing and it will be established! I believe with my heart and do not doubt that you are more than able to bring to pass every decree I make. With bold expectation, I put a demand on heaven to perform. *I proclaim by my authority in Christ Jesus that:* I am the head and not the tail. I have dominion over the tactics and devices of my enemies. My covenant with God includes provision and protection. I will not be in lack another day in my life. Abundance dwells within my borders. Every generational curse attached to the blood in my veins, my health, finances, relationships, and ministry is canceled right now in Jesus' name! I seal the door that gave them legal access to my life. I uproot every demonic seed planted. I live under an open heaven, and favor is attracted to me. I will establish kingdom wherever I go. My enemies are my footstools. Ambushments are in my enemies' camps. I pursue and sow peace. Therefore I reap peace. I am His instrument of righteousness. He always causes me to triumph. I will experience divinely open doors that no man can shut. Divine connections will locate me. Now let God be glorified and Satan be horrified! In Jesus' Name, AMEN!

PROCLAMATIONS OF WAR

2 Chronicles 20:15 (KJV)

And he said, Hearken ye, all Judah, and ye inhabitants of Jerusalem, and thou king Jehoshaphat, Thus saith the Lord unto you, Be not afraid nor dismayed by reason of this great multitude; for the battle is not yours, but God's.

Exodus 14:13 (KJV)

And Moses said unto the people, Fear ye not, stand still, and see the salvation of the Lord, which he will shew to you today: for the Egyptians whom ye have seen today, ye shall see them again no more forever.

Joshua 24:15

And if it seem evil unto you to serve the Lord, choose you this day whom ye will serve; whether the gods which your fathers served that were on the other side of the flood, or the gods of the Amorites, in whose land ye dwell: but as for me and my house, we will serve the Lord.

Further Study: Psalm 106:7-8

FINAL WORD

"The war is lost or won on the battlefield of the mind. Therefore, we must consistently think the thoughts of victory."

~Lionel J Traylor~

FINAL THOUGHTS

Spiritual warfare at its first attempt is the enemy's desire to influence the thinking of the saint in a negative and perverse manner. That's right, the initial battleground is your mind. The enemy does this through the power of suggestion. Insinuation, false perception, lies, and gossip are all tools used to penetrate the ear gate into the soul. Once the seed is planted, it must quickly be uprooted. If not, this cursed weed will begin to grow and choke out "The Fruit of the Spirit" until all that is left is a barren tree, bearing only briers, thorns, and thistles. And for this cause, we cannot afford to be ignorant or passive regarding spiritual warfare. It offends God when we operate beneath who we are purposed to be and settle for a life shrouded in fear and defeat. Christ has given us authority over *all* the power of the enemy (Luke 10:19). So, go forth praise, pray, prophesy and proclaim! Charge on toward your victory, knowing that there are *No Losses, Only Lessons*!

WAR KEY

When to speak is just as important as
what to speak and who to speak to.
Some things are better unspoken.
Some things are to see and pray.
Some things are to see and prepare.
Some are to see and PROCEED.

WAR KEY

If we preach biblical obedience without the biblical blessings of obedience, we are teaching the faithful to engage in a warfare that has no benefits or reward."

WAR KEY

"In warfare, the first and most vital attack is always COMMUNICATIONS. If you cannot communicate, the ENEMY has already won the battle."

WAR KEY

"The Mind is the most pivotal place for engaging
in Spiritual Warfare. And though you may lose a
battle or two... Doesn't mean you have
to lose the war."

WAR KEY

"There are some battles you were not anointed to fight... you were anointed to STAND!"

WAR KEY

"Some people are not WORTH the title ENEMY in your life. To engage in warfare with them is to bring something to them that apparently they no longer have... Value in your life."

WAR KEY

Some wars are not worth the resources spent to fight them. Investigate before you invest. Always ask yourself, "Are the spoils of battle worth engaging this enemy?"

ABOUT THE AUTHOR

Lionel J. Traylor is one of the most influential voices of faith in our time. With an unwavering mandate from God, Lionel J. Traylor's mission has been to establish the kind of ministry that is devoted to restoring communities, serving the impoverished, restoring families, and strengthening individuals within the body of Christ locally, nationally, and worldwide. Bishop Traylor is a renowned and respected spiritual leader, reformer, and trend-setter for change in both the religious and secular arena. His sound teaching, fatherly coaching, and ability to mold leaders are transforming the world. He is the founder of The Epicenter Church, a progressive ministry which serves hundreds of worshipers weekly and is positioned in the heart of Jackson, MS. He has preached the Gospel nationwide and has shared platforms with national and international speakers and leaders, appearing on both TBN and The Word Network, respectively.

With over two decades of ministry, marriage, and eight wonderful kids between them, the Traylors are favored by God and have been positioned for greatness.